Dancing for the
MOON

written by
Alexandra Steeves

illustrated by
Julie Grechukh

In the dark of the night,

The moon shines a light.

Casting a glow,
On your dancing show.

When the music plays,

Your body SWAYS.

And then to the beat,
You STOMP your feet.

The moon looks to see,
And with a one, two, three...

You start with some SPINS,
And your dance begins!

WIGGLE WIGGLE WIGGLE

The moon lets out a giggle.

TAPPITY-TAP
TAP

The moon starts to clap.

SLIDE
SLIDE
SLIDE

The moon grins wide.

The moon shouts
"HOORAY!"

BEND
BEND
BEND

Now the song's near the end.

It will soon be dawn,
And the moon has a yawn.

You do one final LEAP,

Then the moon's off to sleep.

Now you're feeling dozy.

So you find somewhere cozy.

And you close your eyes,
As the sun starts to rise.

For Will. To the moon... - A.S.

Dancing for the Moon

© 2022 Alexandra Steeves

Text by Alexandra Steeves
Book design by Alexandra Steeves
Illustrations by Julie Grechukh

www.alexandrayoung.ca

ISBN 9798356036460 (print)

Printed on demand.

Other books by Alexandra Steeves:

Hazel and Her Nut
Penelope the Puddle Jumper

Made in the USA
Las Vegas, NV
28 February 2023

68238974R00017